Five Pears or Peaches

Five Pears or Peaches

Stories by
Reginald Gibbons

Broken Moon Press · Seattle

Earlier versions of some of these stories appeared in the following publications: "Five Pears or Peaches" in *North American Review;* "Hollister Road," "Friday Snow," "No Matter What Has Happened This May," "The Vanishing Point," "Five Pears or Peaches," and "Money," in slightly different form, in *Saints* (Persea Books, 1986); "Mekong Restaurant" in *Missouri Review;* "Hide and Seek" in *The American Voice;* and "Before" in *The American Poetry Review.* "The Vanishing Point" was reprinted in *Chicago Works* (Morton Press, 1990).

Printed in the United States of America.

ISBN 0-913089-23-0
Library of Congress Catalog Card Number: 90-86383

Cover image by Kay Rood. Used by permission of the artist.

Broken Moon Press
Post Office Box 24585
Seattle, Washington 98124-0585 USA

Kate was five.
I had been reading to her from a book,
and had just finished it.

She took the book from me and held it.
Can I have this book? she asked.
Can I have it for my own life?

And salted was my food, and my repose,
Salted and sobered, too, by the bird's voice
Speaking for all who lay under the stars,
Soldiers and poor, unable to rejoice.

Edward Thomas

...to bind up the brokenhearted,
to proclaim liberty to the captives,
and the opening of the prison
to them that are bound.

Isaiah 61:1

Contents

Otter   3

Hide and Seek   5

Five Pears or Peaches   7

Friday Snow   9

Mekong Restaurant   11

Before   15

Courthouse   19

On Belmont   23

Arms   25

The Vanishing Point   27

Mission   31

Forsaken in the City   33

He   35

A Singular Accomplishment   39

Money   41

She   43

Preparations for Winter   47

Three Persons on a Crow   51

Proserpine at Home   53

Dead Man's Things   57

Hollister Road   59

My Dream of Bill   63

No Matter What
Has Happened This May   65

All-Out Effort   67

Five Pears or Peaches

Otter

Stay in the river, Father John told Bill. Stay in the river, don't go over to the bank and climb up there in those weeds, stay out in the middle, go where *it* is flowing. You don't *know* where it is flowing but you have to stay in it, you don't have to know, you can't know. Stay in the river.

But, Bill said. I've been around rivers and streams all my life, I've been up in those weeds and found those fantastic nests in there, with all those eggs, those wonderful nests, that's where I like to be.

But that's only till they hatch, Father John said. That's only for them to leave, so they can get into the river, even the mama leaves that nest as soon as they are born and goes back into the river, you can't stay there.

You stay in the river, don't be afraid of where it's going to carry you, stay in it, that's where you're meant to be.

Hide and Seek

And the youngest child, out of an unnoticed sadness, would sometimes go into the utility room when no one was looking and crawl behind the green curtain and put herself with the dirty shoes and odd tools and other things used sometimes. She would wait for someone to notice her absence, to notice that she was gone, to notice — and then to come looking for her, full of need and alarm. She was waiting for someone to want to find her: Where'd she go? Where is she? Let's find her! Because: we can't go on without her. Because: we love her. Because: we need her *here,* with us all the time. Because: we love her more than anyone else!

But the other children didn't come. They just kept on playing, they weren't going to come, so after a long while she would have to crawl out again; she always did, from this place she had chosen near Daddy's work shoes for around the yard. Mother hadn't liked looking at them there; she was the one who from the shelf above had hung a heavy green curtain to hide that bottom shelf.

Now these many years later I am looking into every room of the house of our lives, looking for you this year and last and always, and just now I have thought of the green curtain that Time has hung over the bottom shelf to hide many things that no one wanted to see, like Work's hard long days. I'm going to creep quietly toward the utility room, and step down the little half step from the kitchen onto the cold linoleum floor, and find you! Here she is! I'll carry you on my shoulders to the living room, where *everyone* is waiting. You're not misery and hardship! You're not old shoes! If you go away from us, we feel everything is cold and diminished. You're the heart of what we have always wanted, and wanted to live for—and we stop everything to find our missing one—without whom we cannot go on—you.

Five Pears or Peaches

Buckled into the cramped back seat, she sings to herself as I drive toward her school through the town streets. Straining upward to see out her window, she watches the things that go by, the ones she sees—I know only that some of them are the houses we sometimes say we wish were ours. But today as we pass them we only think it; or I do, while she's singing—the big yellow one with a roofed portico for cars never there, the pink stucco one with red shutters that's her favorite. Most of what she sings rhymes as it unwinds in the direction she goes with it. Half the way to school she sings, and then she stops, the song becomes a secret she'd rather keep to herself, the underground sweetwater stream through the tiny continent of her, on which her high oboe voice floats through forests softly, the calling of a hidden pensive bird—this is the way I strain my grasp to imagine what it's like for her to be thinking of things, to herself, to be feeling her happiness or fear.

After I leave her inside the school, which was converted from an old house in whose kitchen you can almost still smell the fruit being cooked down for canning, she waves goodbye from a window, and I can make her cover her mouth with one hand and laugh and roll her eyes at a small classmate if I cavort a little down the walk.

In some of her paintings, the sun's red and has teeth, but the houses are cheerful, and fat flying birds with almost human faces and long noses for beaks sail downward toward the earth, where her giant bright flowers overshadow like trees the people she draws.

At the end of the day, her naked delight in the bath is delight in a lake of still pleasures, a straight unhurried sailing in a good breeze, and a luxurious trust that there will always be this calm warm weather, and someone's hand to steer and steady the skiff of her. Ashore, orchards are blooming.

Before I get into bed with her mother at night, in our house, I look in on her and watch her sleeping hands come near her face to sweep away what's bothering her dreaming eyes. I ease my hand under her back and lift her from the edge of the bed to the center. I can almost catch the whole span of her shoulders in one hand— five pears or peaches, it might be, dreaming in a delicate basket —till they tip with their own live weight and slip from my grasp.

Friday Snow

Something needs to be done—like dragging a big black plastic sack through the upstairs rooms, emptying into it each wastebasket, the trash of three lives for a week or so. I am careful and slow about it, so that this little chore will banish the big ones. But I leave the bag lying on the floor and I go into my daughter's bedroom, into the north morning light from her windows, and while this minute she is at school counting or spelling a first useful word I sit down on her unmade bed and I look out the windows at nothing for a while, the unmoving buildings—houses and a church—in the cold street.

Across it a dark young man is coming slowly down the white sidewalk with a snowshovel over his shoulder. He's wearing only a light coat, there's a plastic showercap under his navy blue knit hat, and at a house where the walk hasn't been cleared he climbs the steps and rings the doorbell and stands waiting, squinting sideways at the wind. Then he says a few words I can't hear to the storm door that doesn't open, and he nods his head with the kindly farewell that is a habit he wears as disguise, and he goes back down the steps and on to the next house. All of this in pantomime, the way I see it through windows closed against winter and the faint sounds of winter.

My daughter's cross-eyed piggy bank is also staring out blankly, and in its belly are four dollar bills that came one at a time from her grandmother and which tomorrow she will pull out of the corked mouth-hole. (It's not like the piggy banks you have to fill before you empty them because to empty them you have to smash them.) Tomorrow she will buy a perfect piece of small furniture for her warm well-lit dollhouse where no one is tired or weak and the wind can't get in.

Sitting on her bed, looking out, I didn't see the lame neighbor child, bundled-up and out of school and even turned out of the house for a while, or the blind woman with burns or the sick veteran—people who might have walked past stoop-shouldered with what's happened and will keep happening to them. So much limping is not from physical pain—the pain is gone now, but the leg's still crooked. The piggy bank and I see only the able young man whose straight back nobody needs.

When he finally gets past where I can see him, it feels as if a kind of music has stopped, and it's more completely quiet than it was, an emptiness more than a stillness, and I get up from the rumpled bed and smooth the covers, slowly and carefully, and look around the room for something to pick up or straighten, and take a wadded dollar bill from my pocket and put it into the pig, and walk out.

Mekong Restaurant

 What is the half-life of a city?

There are green shoots of rice, a soft diaphanous green undulating, shimmering, in a breeze over the flat surface of water, outside a village of tiny frail huts with talk in them, under trees of a rainy hot climate, washed in rain, in a country of rainclouds and war.

A menu in Vietnamese and English.

A dozen immigrants waiting among native and naturalized citizens for their boxes and bags inside a terminal at O'Hare. Refugees have streamed back the way the last war came—into the very country that had turned the fire on them. With them they've brought their children and their names. Some of their children; some of their parents; names that must struggle to be pronounced inside unfamiliar mouths.

But these streets blow with a wind of ice. Or, in summer, they show a jewel glitter sparkling like sequins on fields of green and gray—innumerable bits of shattered glass on raw vacant lots between crumbling apartment blocks and ramshackle three-flats. Up and down the busy street there are shops, Viet Hoa Market, Nha Trang Restaurant, Video King, White Hen, Viet Mien Restaurant, McDonalds, Dr. Ngo Phung Dentist, Nguyen Quang

Attorney At Law, Viet My Department Store. High and far as mountains beyond and above the two-story roofs of this street the winter gray-on-white cityscape wears banners of steam flapping straight sideways in the bitter wind. If you stare at the big buildings long enough you might begin to sense a fundamental instability in the balanced masses of stone and you might wonder why they don't just fall.

Go out into a park field and hide under a weed.

Same moon, not the same moon. After danger and escapes, after feeling so intensely the desire to live, to live in such a place will make some feel they have come to their own funeral. To live away from your own place, to live far away from your own place, and to think you will never return, is to be condemned to have been saved one time too many, some will feel. When meteor showers fall next summer, you won't see them because the underbelly of the sky is lit orange all night in every season. But the children are growing accustomed.

An immigrant boy of fourteen wearing black trousers and a white shirt and a thin jacket is standing with his immigrant parents at the counter of the high school office, waiting to be called in to be registered; the clerks are busy, paying the immigrants no mind, and the mother and father and boy are waiting. At this school the students speak twenty-nine native tongues, or thirty-four, or sixty-five.

One hears stories of the city. Some legendary summer evening of thirty years ago, across the deep street chasm from the important, wealthy, powerful white men in the twenty-fifth-floor Tavern Club, among the columns of the little Greek rotunda top ornament on the twentieth-something-floor roof on the other side of Michigan Avenue, hired for this occasion, some white women wearing only very diaphanous gowns, specially floodlit, unreachable, danced while the club members ate their evening meal. Most of the money is in the white people's hearts; most of the fear is in the black people's pockets.

The year lasts longer here. It is a proven fact: of quantum physics: that time passes more slowly when the air is cold than when it is warm, and that ice is radioactive. (Near here is a famous atom smasher surrounded by scientists.)

Near here also are two zoos, many banks, millions of persons, and the inland sea, frozen for a long way out, and hills of ice that have risen along the beaches, and blackened piles and heaps of decayed snow beside the lake-front roads where the traffic is always speeding by.

A menu in English and Vietnamese.

It's late, he's looking out, from beside the raging stove, through the kitchen pick-up window, at the way it is now, at three American strangers, still in their overcoats, who have come in, who are looking around, who are sitting down hesitantly at a table.

What is the half-life of a city?

Before

It was late morning, and in the late morning the apartment is quiet. All three beds have been left unmade, dirty dishes from the night before lie in the kitchen sink, two damp towels clutter the floor of the little bathroom, and the front door is locked on a daytime stillness.

Before this, before the rush to leave, even before anyone woke, what was there? There was peace in the five rooms on the second floor. Into each of the three dreaming souls the sounds of the spring daylight had begun to enter: the singing town birds roused in trees and bushes—robins, starlings, sparrows, and a triumphant cardinal whistling from the top of a telephone pole—and the first few cars starting, and an early plane above the town.

Before that, before anyone had slept, lying in bed face to face, man and woman had closed their eyes, had lain still, aware along their bodies of each other's warmth and solidity in the dimness, exhausted, remedyless, greedy for at least the least contentment of having gone past the time for work or thought, lying separate and half asleep in the some comfort of each other's arms.

Before that, before anyone had gone to bed, there was the sound of a child crying—their little child who cried so long in bed, who called his crying so far that when at last he ceased and was calm, not yet helped but too tired to keep crying, from next door came the sound of another child crying, child who had heard his call and, shaken by it, was relaying it on, unable not to, carrying the search for an answer farther down the street.

Before that, it had been bedtime—some anguish unknowable by the man or woman twisting the child's face, wringing tears and wailing from him. An obsessing heart might falter at such helpless sadness. And the mother's shoulders are too heavy, they weigh her down into a chair, the father stands pained and weak, in danger of becoming angry, his face failing for lack of a remedy.

Before that, there had been television and before that, dessert, and before that, dinner. All the while the little boy was struggling to escape a fear he can't explain to them; but not until later will it come for him, will it come close to him and seem about to surround him, will it grab him with its horrible hands, will it eat him, will it *have* him. And they don't know about that, they don't understand it, he can't say it because he can't even quite think it.

Before that, there had been the man's arrival home, tired and looking as if some of his very substance had been worn from him again by the day's work. In the aisles of supermarkets, one after another, he had stood, with one painful shoe unlaced, resting that foot on edge, his hand marking the long sheets on his clipboard, his eyes counting things and things. At his entrance into their realm, the realm of woman and child, he had put on some cheer for them, and lifted the timid boy up in his arms and hugged him, and felt the child's small precious hands at the back of his neck; and he had remembered to ask what he could of the woman's day and he had tried to listen to her and he had thought of a dozen things he would have liked to tell her if he could have found the words, if long before now he could have found the words—so that they would have been ready when he needed them. But it was too late to start looking for them. And could he hope that she would care to hear him beyond her own cares, which weighed on him, too?

Before that, the woman had thought about how to speak to the man, about what to say, what to ask, how to ask it, how to hope he would answer, how to make a beginning of a beginning of a change, how to figure out what it was that could be changed, that needed to be changed, how to change it, how to find a place to stand to start, inside these rooms, clothes, hopes. How to find the corner where the dissonance sounded, when it did, and go there and make it harmonious. How to identify whatever it was that was not what it should be, how to overcome tiredness and habit, the child's anxiousness, the weight of her own sense of a responsibility too great, of all the consciousness that together they lived, but that seemed to be hers alone to feed and warm and prod into speech—that simple overwhelming *how*, over a cup of coffee and a cigarette while the little boy, at long long last, and for only a little late-afternoon while, napped.

Before that, on the small round table in their bedroom, in a quiet moment of the day when woman and child had been elsewhere together, a faded sentimental tablecloth had lain smooth where it had been carefully smoothed for a lamp and a book, had hung half a foot irregularly over the edge all around, its grapes and leaves and red border in still, tumbled pleats. The lamp was made out of an empty clear glass one-gallon wine jug, with a yellow burlap shade that insisted on a mood of cheer; and the book had been left artfully to one side, awaiting an unknown person's, some visitor's, charmed kiss of attention or changed life, that would at the same moment be felt by the woman whose hand, a few days before, had left it there with just this unspoken hope. Had lingered over it. But this drama had only been rehearsed, not performed. Later the table would stand silent and still all night after other scenes were played out.

Before that, there were reasons and wishes. There was this and that that had happened. There was the bitter taste of the wish to be able to do some things over again, and there was the honey taste of other memories, to go with the salt. There was, there was. There would always be there was, and never the moment to reach back, to touch lightly—as you might touch a leaf of a houseplant

17

after you had watered it with generosity and helpfulness in your spirit — what had been, to make it grow in just a slightly different direction, somehow, for the sake of the morning that would come spilling light on what merely is, confirming it, ungainsayable it, it in all its unrecoverable antecedent unknowing preparations.

It is late morning. The apartment is empty, all are at their lives again, today, their same lives.

Courthouse

 Once upon a time / there was a little man /
who ate little children.
He had a wife that ate children, too.
Once a little kid came, and got ate up!
"Gee, I've eaten a lot of kids!"
They made a gate with the bones.
And the bones got bigger and bigger.
Some of the bones was so big that *nobody* jumped over them.
Only the person that made the bones, and it was God.
He made the bones littler and littler and littler.
Then people could jump over them.
The man that ate little children—he died.
Suddenly the woman died.
They're lucky they had a little kid.
So he could save their house.
He had money, and bought a new house.
That was made out of gold.

Your honor, testimony of this sort proves absolutely nothing
at all.

Over and over the little boy drew a snowman. And said of it,
It has hair in its mouth, it has hair in its mouth. He was the boy
who at three had been beaten and taken by a teacher's aide into
the school bathroom where she pulled the door shut and she

pushed him down on herself. But when he was drawing the snow-man and saying, It has hair in its mouth, nobody would understand. He was not trying to tell them something. He was telling them something. Why didn't they say they understood?

Where you wait to be called, first they screen a high-school slide show, recapping a false history from revolutionary days to the present, showing cartoons of aspects of the justice system, then photos of the modern courthouse with mild rock music as soundtrack. "YOU: THE JUROR," says the amplified male military voice, "NINETY PERCENT OF ALL JURY TRIALS IN THE WORLD TAKE PLACE IN AMERICA. THESE ARE THE PEOPLE WHO WORK IN THE COURTROOM, WHO YOU WILL SEE—THE JUDGE, THE CLERK, THE COURT REPORTER, THE ATTORNEYS AND LITIGANTS (THE PROSECUTOR SITS NEAREST THE JURY, WITH THE PLAINTIFF IN A CIVIL CASE), THE WITNESSES, AND YOU, THE JUROR.

"PAY CLOSE ATTENTION TO EACH WITNESS WHO TESTIFIES, DO NOT MAKE ANY INVESTIGATIONS OF YOUR OWN INTO THE CASE, THE OPENING STATEMENTS AND FINAL STATEMENTS ARE NOT EVIDENCE, THE JUDGE WILL INSTRUCT YOU CONCERNING RELEVANT POINTS OF LAW."

There will be peremptory dismissal and dismissal for cause, there will be the swearing of the jury, and the jury deliberations, and the verdict, and the Battle Hymn of the Republic, "...A CITIZEN, AN HONORABLE MAN OR WOMAN, A *JUROR!*"

From the Dan Ryan Expressway and the TriState Tollway, from the Gold Coast and Evanston, into this building come three hundred judges. Do they arrive in carriages with livery? Do trumpets sound? And, in a year, seven million pieces of litigation. And then in the jury room the three color TVs come on, with loud game shows, and then you wait the rest of the morning, and at noon the soap operas come on, and in them people are blackmailing each other, killing each other, stealing from each other, hating and tormenting and hitting each other with their words or their fists, coloring each other various shades of green and purple, noticing each other's clothes, shouting and intravenous and wretched and relaxed and low-calorie and crying. Even there, however, no one has mauled a child.

Hyenas prowl beyond the margins of the herd, always ready to take a small one.

A little hand points, not very precisely, at a person sitting behind a wooden table.

In fact, Your Honor, the pointing was very inconclusive, even though my client was looking right *at* the child!

The other day, when I asked you to tell me a story, and you told me about the man who ate children up, was that really about somebody you know?
No.
Why did you draw the snowman?
I didn't draw no snowman.

Thank you for serving in the one-day, one-trial system.

Home again, home again, jiggety jig.

On Belmont

Watch it! brother, he said, who had come up beside me without my even noticing it as I was walking on crowded Belmont late one summer night. He had already dropped into a squat, half-leaning against the building wall, a brown-bagged bottle in one hand. Get down, he warned me.

Ragged, stoned, looking full of fear. I stopped near him.

I don't think I had heard even a backfire.

Machine guns, he said. I know, I was *there,* he said, turning his head from side to side.

Not machine guns, I said, to be helpful. Then I had what I thought was a good idea. I said, And even if it is, they're a long way from here. (They'd *have* to be, suppose it *was* possible, they were still blocks away from here, at least, off down the busy late-hours streets lit too bright. We had plenty of time.)

Oh, he said; meaning, Is that what you think? With a quick glance. His gaze sidelong, but strong. It would take too long to teach me. But he explained: That's when they're really bad, that's when they get you, when they're far away.

He stayed low, one knee half up, squatting on the other thigh, protecting the bottle held half behind him. He looked up and down the street. I waited as long as I could, maybe half a minute, but all this was over now, that was about as far as we could take it, now that we had had our moment of contact in this world, after the accumulated years when separately we had wandered other streets and other countries. We had happened to be momentarily side by side at the sound of whatever it had been, maybe a gun. I started on down Belmont, and got back my pace, I was heading for the train.

Maybe to him, still squatting and leaning there, not yet ready to stand up, or able, it seemed like he was the one who would get to where things made sense and were safe, and I was walking foolishly in a place of danger. How could he explain it to me, it was way too late for me and everybody like me.

Arms

 In Chicago, in the single display window of a used record store where teenagers not much beyond childhood hang out, they've put a discarded department-store mannikin, or rather the upper two-thirds of one. They put a summer nightgown on her that's thin and lacy, the length of which lies rumpled on the grubby floor at her cut-off hips as if the hem has risen on water she'd stepped into—thinking of doing what? On the surface of the same pool some dusty album covers are floating around her.

Appropriately, her head is bowed, her eyes are cast downward, you can't see her face because they've also draped a large piece of delicate white fabric over her head like an oversize bridal veil—is it a kind of unwitting parody of such a veil?—and it hangs down as far as her breasts and a little lower. And, also, she has no arms.

A clothed, unintended allusion to the statue of the Venus de Milo, woman with no arms or legs, you might be tempted to say. The trouble is that that connection, rather than investing the mannikin with some added significance that a few of us can catch (and at which we feel a pleasant self-approval)—that connection between this mannikin and the ancient salvaged figure actually throws its light in the other direction. Starkly it shows what it is that the Venus de Milo represents in her broken state, disfigured in a way that has for so long, and so cozily, lain in the psyche of acquirers and connoisseurs and found approval there.

25

How can I say this, and the rest of this?

There's the attraction of the beautiful powerless body. Powerless when represented without arms; powerless when it is the small body of one who, without having lost arms and legs, is nonetheless defenseless and a kind of prey to others.

I'm not trying to convince. I only want to tell you what I see: a day doesn't pass now when the experts aren't writing books and explaining to juries about little crayon drawings of children, drawn by children, after things you can imagine, do I have to say it?, and almost always the children draw themselves without arms.

The Vanishing Point

A young man with very bad teeth and a wall-eyed gaze, holding some poster boards on his lap, where they sagged at each side, and drawing on the top one with an old chewed ballpoint pen.

It was a severely rectilinear highway scene: a powerful exaggerated vanishing point puckering the empty horizon, lanes of cars coming on—as yet only outlined—and lanes of big trucks going away, already finished. One after another, all alike, semi-trailers with company names on them, and all the perspective acutely correct. It all looked to have been drawn with a ruler, strictly and slowly; but he was doing it freehand, each stroke of the pen absolutely precise. Or rather, as imprecise as the human hand, but with an authority that could convey and even create precision in your eyes as you looked. Even the lettering he was putting on the side of the last, closest, largest trailer was as if painted by machine, and he never paused to consider proportions or angles, but simply kept drawing and darkening the shapes with the blue pen, as if he were tracing with quick uncanny dash a faint design already there on the white floppy board.

This was at Chicago and State, in the subway station.

A woman happened to come stand near him, and watched as he worked with his intent rhythm, his head bobbing and sometimes with his face low to study his work closely with one eye at a time. She watched, and he noticed her and smiled a wreck-toothed wide blind man's smile at her, and said, more than asked, "Nice

27

work, idn't it!" She put her right thumb up and smiled back at him, and said nothing, and he lifted the top board and showed her the finished one underneath, for an instant—another roadscape, in colors, filled in and alive, the whole huge white board crammed with convincing and convinced detail.

"Nice work, idn't it!" he said again, and showed her the one underneath that one. Again, thumb up, and she too smiled happily —a wholly natural acknowledgment of him, an unsurprised understanding of his talent. She didn't act as if it seemed strange to her that he was sitting on a worn drab bench on the subway platform, next to the tracks, working in the dim light while commuters and others stood around waiting impatiently for the next train. It didn't seem to strike her that he was crazy and half-blind. That his work was driven, obsessively scrupulous, uninhabited, repetitive, brilliant, rhythmical, depthless, spiritless, useless.

"Nice work, idn't it!" he said to her each time, and he showed her—and me, because I too was standing there—six or eight more drawings: the Sears Tower, the skyline along Michigan Avenue, traffic in the streets, not a single person. The long lines were perfectly straight but when you looked at them more carefully they zigged with freehand force across the board in spurts. And her thumb went up to each in turn, and she smiled and each time she did, he said, "Nice work, idn't it!"

"I do nice work!" he said. "I did *all* these, and not a *single mistake!* Nice work!" he was saying as the train came in like sandpaper, hissing and blasting. She walked away toward it, without saying goodbye, and he looked at me, then. "Nice work, idn't it!" he said, as cheerfully as a man could ever say it.

"It's beautiful!" I said. The doors to the train opened a few feet away and everyone was stepping inside. "It's nice *work!*" he said, smiling, and I moved to the train and stepped in, the great force in him holding me to him still, and with part of myself I wished that it would win, but I did get in, the last passenger, and the doors shut and immediately the train jerked and began to roll out of the station and away.

Mission

After she had been in her first school for months already, one afternoon at home she was crying because of something a friend had done or maybe only said to her, and I was trying to offer some solace, some distraction, when she nearly shouted all of a sudden, "You and Mommy left without even saying goodbye to me!" I said—shocked to have caused a wound so lingering that other pain must inevitably lead back to it—"When?"

"The first day of kindergarten," she said, and she really began to wail, looking up at the ceiling, tears pouring from her, her face crumpling.

"But you wanted us to leave! You were lined up with the other kids to go into class behind the teacher, I thought you were happy to go in!"

"But the other parents were still there! And you left without even saying goodbye!" she said. The way rain can arrive with a violent flurry of pouring and thunder but then settles into a steady fall that is the real rain, that will after a while flood gutters and basements and streets and fields and rivers till there's damage it will take time to repair—so she settled wearily and deeply into her crying.

However a wound was caused, it is already there, it can't be undone, it needs to be healed.

My child is standing before me on the steps down to the back door, her eyes level with mine as I sit on a higher step holding

31

both her hands, and she is crying as if she will never stop, and the friend's slight is forgotten, the first day of kindergarten is forgotten, there is deeper sorrow than that, incomprehensible and punishing, and for now I am pouring over her the unslakeable longing and helpless protective presentiment that bind me irremediably to her in love, and I understand again what I must do as long as she and I live, and how much I want to do this, to love her, and need to, and how too it is not enough. It is in the way of things, and no blame on anyone for it, that it is not enough.

Forsaken in the City

On the crowded street, under the tenements and apartments tilted over sidewalk shops, in the middle of people choosing apples and cabbages and potatoes from stacked wooden crates and wicker baskets outside the grocers' doorways, what noise—while others inside are gathering butter and milk and cheese and loaves of bread in their arms, jammed against the counters to pay, clamoring and waiting. On the corner, the afternoon newspapers stacked at the feet of a man calling the headline; the smell of exhaust and ripe fruit and, from the cheap restaurants, frying oil. And past all the cars stuck in the mid-city traffic inching homeward, whose horns blast and bleat up the echoing man-made canyons, here and there amid the roar is hidden the stillness before motion resumes and the stillness after it has stopped, both stillnesses ceaselessly arriving and dissolving again into noise, in this person's sudden halting before a beautiful eggplant, in that one's closed eyes while standing at the bus stop. And this man on his way through, this one person among all the others who thinks he has just heard his name called out, quite clearly, turns and looks back over his shoulder. He didn't think he knew anyone around here, he looks across the street, peers into the open doorways nearby to find who it is if it is anyone who knows him in this hubbub. The sound sparkled like a gem discovered among pebbles in a shallow clear stream and it caught him abruptly and made him forget what he'd been thinking. But he doesn't hear his name called again, no one looks familiar, he must

33

have heard it in some other name or call, some play of sound that his mind seized mistakenly from the noise to make the similar seem the identical. Did he hear it because without any awareness of his feelings he had wanted to be called, to be summoned? It was his childhood name, a name for all of his hidden being, not the name anyone who knows him now calls him by, and he looks here and there and sees no one he might know from back then, no one he recognizes. He could look up and see above the street the faces in windows: in this one and that, someone is leaning. The late afternoon's hot and in that window or this comes a glimpse of someone inside moving across a darkened, still room. And above them are the roofs with no one on them at all except for one strange creature with wings who seems disappointed; turning back from the edge, where she was standing only an instant before, looking down, her call still echoing, she is about to take flight.

He

 Oh let's say that the great tree that the storm blew down will be set upright and will grow again.

The wind that pushed it down will stand it up again. Let's say. You can do it. The storm wasn't that bad, you're OK. You just put it behind you, that's all.

Cars are mysterious things. And women.

What I feel is *my* business, and my friends understand me, Chick and Frank and Derek, OK?

What do you want me to say?

Look, maybe I don't make that much. (Look, I make a lot of dough.) But there's one thing I *can* do.

Let's get that meat on the grill. Let's bust their heads. Let's get up for it. Let's go for it. Let's do it.

Hold your fist up higher, to each side of your face, no, wider, good. That way you can deflect my jab, see? No, like this, see, you don't try to stop it, you push it away and it goes right past you. Right. Now you're getting it.

Combative. The invention of theory; fortune; it's the principle of the thing; *all* I said was; fight (sport, spectatorship, partisanship, gambling, money, hierarchy, dominion, betrayal, blood, bloodshed, territory, noblesse, speed, strength, limelight) or flight; bend or break; rough it, get moving, pack some heat; working

35

lunch, telemetry, building with stone; pulpits, benches, chairs, seats, coffins; and for each of these, some opposite or other.

Recently been elected to the prestigious the management and research team which built it up took it public and then sold the successful on the hobby side of things Geoff has kept up with his painting V.P. of Information Systems proud father of Sean. Laid off when orders fell carried the piano just with Jim over to Sally's house in his pickup it was two months then three then four and started spending most of his time at Louise's, we wouldn't even see him till late cases of beer got cheese, his wife did anyway, from the food line. Hardwood floors, 3 bedrooms, 2 baths, overhead bluejeans, 12-gauge boots, workbench, riding mower, even a boat.

Aiee! Buy, CAT-scan, dentures, E-mail, fantasies, gunpowder, hyperconductivity, internal combustion, lift-off, missionary, neurosis, O-rings, prayer breakfast, sell, torque, wages — the challenge, the network, the commission, yes! But: hernia, ulcers, heart, emphysema, arthuritis, baldness, hangovers, bad back, prostate, hypertension, the big C, widows.

Term life, annual interest, liability and collision, still under warranty, commute, the boy's games at school, new whatever for the wife, TV sports, the daughter's hopeless boyfriends, consolidate with a single loan, indoor-outdoor carpet, and did you ever notice how the labels on things at the hardware store are so plain and functional, no fancy wrappers, just a label telling what it is and how to install it? That's so male. That's male packaging. I mean, compare *Vogue* to *Popular Mechanics* or Laura Ashley to True Value! Coleman, Shakespeare, Black and Decker, Daiwa, John Deere, Sears, you see what I mean? Wirecutters and computers, carburetion and wattage, price-per and per-hundredweight. Any sort of measurement, for that matter.

To say nothing of 117 to 115, 42 to 27, 3 to zip, two kings and three fives. All that striving drives the lives and dries the wives. Gimme that. *You* say. Crash and burn. That's all she wrote. Yee-haw. Fuck you.

A Singular Accomplishment

 Laz Hart used to be able to put his toe in his mouth while he was standing up, could still do that when he was a man, and used to make everybody laugh thataway. He's eighty-or-so, now, he preached Daddy's funeral sermon, thirty or forty years ago, didn't you know that?

And when we were near the Old House we drove by a neighbor's, an old man was out front puttering at the aluminum rowboat he'd somehow put up on the roof of his car, although it didn't seem like much of a day for fishing, with the weather coming in dark and fast. It was Laz, and Jim stopped our pickup and called out to him, and he came over to the window. He nodded and said hello and kidded Jim about being back in the old neighborhood, where old-time cutthroats and renegades remain a favorite local legend, especially among those whose lives have been lawful and mild for as many as eighty years or more.

The matter of Laz's old antics came up, his putting his toe in his mouth. Abruptly he stepped back a few paces, his baggy overalls flapping around his bony age in the green gusty wind before rain, and he reached down to his huge laced boots and pulled one foot right up to his face, standing straight up, and put the toe of his boot to his teeth, grimacing with a smile, and when we stared at him full of surprise, and couldn't think of what to say, he put it down again and backed away with a bashful pride, as if he, the retired preacher, had just invented the very wheel of human civilization but wished not to take too much credit for it.

Money

 The children are eating lunch at home on a summer weekday when a man comes to the door and asks their mother if she has anything that needs fixing or carrying or any yardwork he can do. They chew their food a little dreamily as, with her back straight and her voice carefully polite, she says No, thank you, I'm sorry, and the man goes away. Who was that, Mama? they say. Oh, no one, she says.

They are sitting down to dinner but they have to wait because the doorbell rings and a thin young boy begins to tell their father about a Sales Program he's completing for a scholarship to be Supervisor, and he holds up a filthy tattered little booklet and lifts also his desperate guile and heavily guarded hope, and the children's father says No thank you sorry but I can't help you out this time, and the boy goes away. The children start to eat and don't ask anything, because the boy was just a boy, but their father acts irritated and hasty when he sits back down.

Once a glassy-eyed heavy girl who almost seems asleep as she stands outside their door offers for sale some little handtowels stitched by the blind people at the Lighthouse for the Blind and the children are in the folds of their mother's full, pleated skirt listening to the girl's small voice and their mother says, Well, I bought some the last time.

She buys the children school supplies and food, she pays the two boys for mowing the yard together and weeding her flower bed. She gets a new sewing machine for her birthday from the

41

children's father, and she buys fabric and thread and patterns and makes dresses for the girls, to save money. She tells the children each to put a dime or quarter into the collection plate at Church, and once a month she puts in a little sealed white envelope, and the ushers move slowly along the ends of the pews weaving the baskets through the congregation, and the organist plays a long piece of music.

Whisk brooms, magazine subscriptions, anything you need hauled away, little league raffle tickets, cookies, chocolate candy, can I do any yard work again and again, hairbrushes, Christmas cards, do you need help with your ironing one time, and more, came calling at the front door while the children were sometimes eating, sometimes playing. Their faces would soften with a kind of comfort in the authority of mother or father, with a kind of wonder at the needy callers.

Their father left for work every day early, and came home for dinner, and almost always went again on Saturday; in his car. Their mother opened a savings account for each child and into each put the first five dollars. The children felt proud to see their names in the passbooks. They wanted to know when they could take the money out, but they were told they had to save their money not spend it.

They felt a kind of pleasure in these mysteries, to know that there were things you would understand later when you grew up and had your own house and while your children were eating their dinner and making too much noise the way you did, you knew it was true, the doorbell would ring, the familiar surprise of it, who would it be, and someone would be holding a little worn book or a bundle of dishtowels or once an old man, but perhaps he only looked old, with his beard, came with bunches of carnations, white, red, and pink, and he too was turned away.

She

(Fruit, kindling, milk, nuts, corn.)

Distaff, credit card, henna, black cloth, perfume, needle, glove, evil eye, nail polish, car keys, purdah, grocery list, stockings, blood, veil, pyre. But we must have an audience for these, and it won't be men, exactly. Creatures of this world — beetles, night birds, moths, tree frogs, crickets, leaves, outside cats, field mice, stars, clouds, and whatever I am. We approach your house, and the side window is humming with brightness. (And a violence that is always there but which nobody sees, like something that has always just happened already but has left no mark, except that in the air there's an echo, like the idea of a cry of weariness.)

The lamplight pushes a pale leaning column out through the panes onto the lawn. We look in at your bright body hesitating a moment on the rug, a glass in your hand.

There's a kind of funnel in the skies overhead that drains down into these rooms the residue of habits, prayers, curfews; brings barred windows, riding sidesaddle, knowing what everything in mother's bureau is; brings baking and birth. Now you call your own daughter and go upstairs, and we rise outside to a higher window, to look in on you again. More and more of us are coming to see you and believe.

Sitting half-dressed with your daughter behind you, you close your eyes as the little girl pulls gently at your hair with a heavy brush, slowly. Long hair that was pinned up. The two small hands make three strands and braid them into one: wife, husband, daughter. Then the girl leaves the room, and your sleepy form half-slumps by the mirror.

Inside the closet near you, like a block of lead on the floor, a metal safe-box holds the deed to the house, the bankbooks, your mother's will, the little girl's first drawings, and the ordinary archives you've kept on behalf of the preoccupied man. Over the box the dresses sweep back and forth like willow branches in a rainy breeze.

At the dinner table, the little girl reads out her school composition, which was different from those of the boys: *The earth as it spins makes a wooshing sound but on earth the sound is different. You can taste the earth, the muddy taste of earth the smoggy taste of smog or smoke they also can be smelled.*

She rises to your rewarding hand like a cat. She has painted her own little nails red. With the comfort of your touch, her eyes close for a second. Then the husband speaks of a friend at work — he hasn't said anything about the girl's composition — who has given him his old coat. He gets up and brings it and hands it to you and the little girl pokes quickly into the pockets but there's nothing in them. Patched at one cuff by a woman unknown to you, a wife who has been replaced, the coat has brought her care here to this house, and you see it. You think of her finger in a thimble, pushing the needle through the tough thick cloth. Her forgotten gesture for a man can fill your hands with light as you hold the coat up and brush its battered weave. Will all that you have done, like her work, fill someone else's black trunk with discarded attentions, and will mere noise drown out the times you have said all right and let me do it and yes?

What was her name?

I don't know. I never thought I should ask him. I didn't meet him for the first time till after he was already married again.

Some memories of an anger held back, of slights, of arguments abandoned because there was no point pursuing them, arguments resolved by fatigue, of disappointments, rise in you as if from wherever she is now this woman could add her troubles to yours. An accustomed silence. It takes too much effort to say words. The husband picks up some dishes and carries them into the kitchen. Your tongue is a small creature rocking in its cage.

From outside, we think your name, it's a kind of calling you. We watch through the window, and with one leg or wing or arm we sweep the air to feel, along with you, your rising from your chair and carrying the coat to the stairs and draping it on the bannister. Obediently it floats up the bannister and glides to lie beside your sewing basket, but neither your husband nor your daughter has seen it go up, and now it is waiting with insatiable comrades for your touch—other clothes, aching small legs, keys, boxes of food and soap, the clothesline, vegetables and meat, switches and buttons, medicine bottles, and that husband's body.

But for now in the living room where you sit down again, the pose: the toe of your right boot in the air (cheap green rainboots you have put on because you're going out), one leg slung over the other, one thigh sealing warmth into the thigh underneath, and the pale hem draped like linen over knees, and the small curving haunch, the torso leaning forward and to one side, the elbow propped on the chair arm, and your hand hidden in your hair that you have loosed again, unable to please yourself with it.

You ready? (He speaks from the kitchen doorway, wiping his hands on a dishtowel, he does help some, give him that much, still in his shirtsleeves.) The babysitter's here, she came to the back door.

Whenever.

The hand leaves your hair, whose hand is it? The cat leaps to your lap, you push it away and it leaps down again.

45

Kisses, hugs; the little one, like you. She doesn't cry much any more when you go out.

Your daughter will grow; your husband will do something.

Whose hand is it that might touch yours? What work might you put your hand to?

There's a way to resist the will of what is, there's a preservation, a rhythm, a selfness, a right thing to do and doable and done.

The bare bulb on the porch comes on, your audience flies quickly back into the night, the wooden front porch in need of painting is the hut at the center, the ark, the shrine of this life. It's the shape of an unrecognized temple where at night your curious worshippers fly to the light (some even to die there). Across it and down the steps move your ordinary feet, which could diminish a nation or bring it justice. But some decree has not yet been cried, there is some failing among creatures, they don't see or they see and don't speak. The waiting of those who only watch you is without power. The power is in you, gathering.

Preparations for Winter

The widow's house—the first widow's house, because there are two of them, side by side—always seemed uninhabited, or with a living stillness at the heart. As if the life inside were far inside, so not even a fingertip touch of it reached the windows. Hidden, retreating, shivering, sheltered, alone.

There was a series of losses. Her parents, you can imagine, long ago in some other era so remote that the light from it, which reaches her only in photos, has shifted to yellow. Then the little community that was once a tiny nation, a neighborhood of odd low brick apartments with, then, pleasant loitering neighbors going in and out of the small shops for meat, dry goods, groceries. (Now the old ones sometimes appear—from where? ghosts are merely persons whose world has so changed it has left them out —and come down the sidewalks once in a while in the summer, and ask the young people up on their porches if they knew so-and-so, who lived there many years, and the young people have never heard of him.) Then the children, who grew up and grew older and grew away. Then her husband, who was beaten with a chair leg in his living room by sadistic invading thieves while she was out.

Then the elm, which had filled the sky so hugely, so solidly and warmly with its slow airy striving bulk. I missed the long labor of their taking it down, their surrounding it and crawling up into it and cutting it to pieces, so its disappearance seemed instant, a kind of bad miracle, and the new light hitting the back of my house, coming through the raw openness, felt cold.

There wasn't any waiting for the unmanageable great stump of the felled tree to soften and decay. It was shredded by mechanical force and violently churned into the earth, as if it had committed a crime against men and what men felt at it was an enormous obliterating rage.

That was a few weeks ago. In her backyard today two men are building a wooden crib for the elm logs. One of the men works ineffectually and dangerously at splitting some of the wood with an axe, having to swing it with a foolish vehemence because he doesn't have a wedge or maul, perhaps doesn't even know he should have one or the other. A young man's careless foolhardiness might offer the widow a preoccupation she could make use of. Even if he's someone she doesn't know, has merely hired, and whom she might fear or distrust. Here he is with his young disregard for his own limbs and life—can you imagine? But she's nowhere in sight.

And didn't anyone—not either of the men, certainly—tell her that elm won't burn, that it's a mistaken economy or convenience to try to use it in her fireplace, that it's wet wood and stinks when it's lit? And that if it died of disease, she mustn't burn it or the smoke will carry its infection to other elms? Who convinced her to have such a solid and well-constructed crib built for worthless wood from her elm? She's been deceived; cheated; led into error.

But perhaps no one needed to talk her into it. Perhaps the two men who don't give a shit for her aren't at all to blame. Perhaps what she gets from them are certain unintended gifts beyond price: the sounds of hammering and a shrill power saw in the still cold air, the smell of sawn lumber, the bright new structure rising deliberately piece by piece. It's all male—the measuring and cutting and making, their flannel work shirts with tears and stains, their old blue jeans, their grunted comments to each other. The elm logs are dark, wet, rough, they're the very lifelessness of the dead tree, still unreduced, intractable, maddeningly astonishingly substantial. As if proof had been required by some executioner, the tree is now proven dead—its parts stacked neatly in the new crib (made of wood), the tree put into a new shape not that of a tree. Then it will be carried into the house by small loads; then mistakenly burned, by God, against its sputtering will to make a warm fire, however foul the smoke, and destroyed into flame and dry ash, not twigs or branches but this very heart of the old elm that presided over every year of the widow's life here. O hearth and carbon. Take the body of the present, unbearable with its wet weight of the past, and wrestle it into the grate and make a fire of dead bone and warm yourself at the cremation. He's dead, he's dead. And all you can accomplish is to spread the dying further.

So she needs something *new* done, even if needless, something that is for a future, even if it's only a future month of cold. Something that will first be new, and then not so new, and then just an ordinary something that like her is going on through the days, as if it always had and always would. She's still nowhere in sight, as they finish their job. She's hidden in her house, waiting. Burn away the old, burn it, make it nothing. Make a last new something.

Three Persons on a Crow

(Oil on Canvas)

It's flying in the wake of first an osprey that has a big fish in its talons and then a gull. Below is a silvery blue river. Somewhere above there might be a thieving eagle that none of them has seen yet, on its way down in a dive to frighten the osprey and then catch the released fish before it falls far down into the river from which it was taken.

On the crow's tail sits the son, last in order of authority but happy with the wildest ride, on stiff feathers planing this way and that as the crow steadies itself in the gusts and drafts. The boy whoops and yells.

His father's riding as if on a horse, sitting on the crow's shoulders with his legs dangling in front of the beating wings. Nearly thrown off with every wing stroke, he's clutching feathers tight with both hands, trying to look brave.

The mother, most vulnerable, most endangered and yet somehow with an air of worthiness and sufficient will, is standing straight up on the crow's head. She doesn't need anything at all to hang onto, she's looking ahead into the wind, at the erratic gull and beyond it the strong osprey clutching the fish, she's acting as if at least some of the catch will be hers, too.

51

Proserpine at Home

 The only spice is salt, there is no ice or coolness, the food she has to prepare is dry, stale, gray. The pantry holds mealy flour, dried beans, hardtack, and hard dried figs that taste of must and sweat. Holes in the dining room floor, big enough for her foot but where she'd better not step, open on a deep bottomlessness, absolutely dark. There even Pluto doesn't go. And in his kitchen sink shit rises when upstairs the toilet's flushed.

No room without a little smoke in it; and beyond the window curtains there's only black emptiness outside, through which the less tormented shades come near the house, floating slowly or sometimes hurtling past, eternal strangers to each other but whispering or moaning to be heard, anyway. So she keeps the curtains closed while she's there; she can scarcely bear to touch them when each year she must move back in, they are so filthy with accumulated smoke and dust and vapor of oil.

The darkness is hot and humid, and in it he works all day, she never asks at what. He doesn't bathe and until she can get used to it again she tries to hold a sleeve or hem of her own—clean at first—over her mouth and nose when she greets him. Even in bed she must cover her face with the bedclothes in order to fall asleep. The sheets are gray despite all the washings she gives them, and black soot spots the gray. The water she must use for washing and cooking is gray. The air seems gray.

Her days—sometimes she merely stares at a small candle flame for hours. She must overhear without wanting to the sounds from outside the house, where she doesn't venture: there is no full voice among all the shades, no resonance of sound in their world, which seems made of shadows and a hot, nearly choking, mist. Pluto himself, although not a shade at all but godly in his way, with his huge physique and exaggerated features, like those of a statue meant to be seen from afar, has an odd voice, small and high. Repeatedly she washes out her clothes and sheets. There is never quite enough light to sew or even cook by, but she must do it anyway. She awaits the passage of days and weeks and months in a realm where each dim hot hour seems a day in itself. Then he comes in suddenly—there are no warning footfalls in a landscape of sooty paths through clouds of dim mists.

His frustration—although, to describe him, "frustration" suggests too much delicacy—is that it's not within his power to inflict any torment great enough on those outside the house to make them go away, and that it's not meant for him to change his rule to the world above. He believes he loves her, and when she's away he pines—although, to describe him, "pines" suggests too much feeling. But he cannot rescue her from the conditions of her life with him, cannot change the half-year string of nights when she cries to herself in a corner, without a window she would want to look out of. In a way, he is almost happier, or at least less troubled, when she is gone and he can only think about her, during the half-year when she is above again and happy and he is still below, at work hammering and tearing ceaselessly without need of rest or change.

When they are together in bed, sometimes she can remember the excitement of his first attentions to her, in another world of air and promises, when she was needy for what he provided. But she must remember also that when she decided at last to refuse him, and her mother agreed that she must, he carried her away by force to keep what he said was already his. Together in the hot darkness, in his house, in his season when she is with him, in bed, what they do is mechanical and efficient and quick, for each of them.

54

Then she gets up and goes to the front room, away from him, and sits in his chair, which he treats as if it were a throne, and she falls asleep there.

And anyway, his strutting, loud, bullying love is incongruously haughty, and would condemn him if there were any eyes besides hers to see it. She does not try to explain to him how she can read his every impulse and thought so easily; he doesn't realize she is far wiser than he. The darkness of his realm is the concealment of his own nature from himself, of his own needs. All the shades are thus estranged from themselves, and he no less than they.

Unlike them, he can feel hope because she must always return, that is the bargain. Yet if, in his tender moments, he would ponder her needs, he cannot see them. Even if he could give her what she wants, he cannot conceive of what that is.

And it embitters her to know that, in the world above, for all her beauty, things were little different; despite her sweetness and her strength, no one there, except her mother, had noticed her or cared a fig for what she wanted or felt. She sits for hours staring at the fragile candle flame. The fig is an oblong or pear-shaped fruit, pulpy when ripe, and eaten raw or preserved or dried with sugar. Green, red, purple, soft, moist, fresh, cool, sweet.

Dead Man's Things

 Well, change from a dead man's pockets, for instance—a quarter was a powerful frightening object to get your hands on if it came from the pocket of a dead man, like the man shot by police whose change spilled onto the sidewalk when he fell, that time at the corner of Main and Polk.

That was much more powerful than the money of a man of no power who wasn't yet dead but only dying, like the Nigerian student who came to Chicago and sold ice cream from a truck in the evenings and who was shot and who, until the police finally came, bled for two hours while some children darted up now and then to take ice cream and money from his truck.

You had a dead man's hat once, bought at a garage sale for two dollars, a beautiful gray Stetson with a rattlesnake-skin band. He hadn't been wearing it when he was killed in a car, and his brother no longer wanted to keep it.

You have some things of a dead man who was your kin and whom you loved because of who he was and what he had done, even though you didn't know him. A small Persian rug, which he bought in 1930-something from a man who came to his door and asked if he'd give him five dollars for it, which he did; that man is long dead now, too.

You have only one thing from his father, which is the way you set the knights on the chessboard, facing in at king and queen, like he taught you when you were about seven or eight.

You have clothes of one dead man—a few things given to you by his son, wearing out now—whom you didn't know well but did admire. When you put something of his on, you sometimes think of him and thank him for helping you onward after he stopped coming with the rest of us. And other clothes—even a coat, the most sacred of all clothing, given to you by the widow of another man who was both a brother and father to you and whom you loved.

Of one of your grandfathers perhaps you have the way you put out your hand when you say certain things, or perhaps even the way you say certain things, who knows, you'll never know, he died when you were two, that one.

And from the man whose coat you wear when it's cold, you have the greatest thing—the very words you speak if you read aloud from his books. The very shape of your breath, and the tempo of your heart as you read, and the space you fall through when his work takes you over and away from everything else, or maybe it's into everything else; and you marvel at what he had and wonder where did he get that, which dead man gave him that or who did he take it from, darting up near him, Beckett or Proust or James or who that lay dying before the police came, and stuffing his pockets with that coin that he held till it was his turn to spend it.

Hollister Road

 Sometimes I wish I had not changed so many times the way I see things, and I could still hold to an earlier way, perhaps one less saddened, slower to guard itself against what it might see.

To recover it even for a moment would require working back in memory and trying to forget my first sight of mountains, from a Greyhound bus in New Mexico, summer I was seventeen. And to reach that point, first I'd have to rid myself of the Pacific Ocean; of scabby-ankled men in broken shoes on hot city streets; of the slave-labor kilns I saw in one far country, and in another, the summer view from a saint's church at dusk when distant village lights started coming on in the valley below; and of all the other images I have preserved, wanting to and no, with a camera in my mind, that are always coming back at unexpected moments and I can't see the connection between where I am, what I'm doing, and all of a sudden what I see.

I would also have to forget the little commercial enterprises and small houses modeled on inappropriate, but perhaps forgivable, grandiosities, that came to crowd our road eventually like warts along the vein of a smooth, plain hand. Everyone was building a house, then. And I would have to restore a field of ordinary weeds, where freeway builders dug a huge straight-sided quarry hole for sand and gravel, a pit so huge that to us it suggested a cataclysm. When they hit clay and stopped digging, it filled with clear greenish water in which nothing ever lived but algae, and finally it had to be called a "lake," and posted against trespassers, when the new houses had come close to it and someone's child, swimming there, had drowned.

I have to go back before all that, to the moment when our house was the last on the road, in a place with few trees, and I can remember some birds—doves, quail, bobwhite, meadowlarks, redbirds. There were killdeer tracks, delicate, as if carefully drawn, in the fine white silt after rain, when the dampness would hold the impression till the hot sun dried everything out again and the dust drifted softly over itself.

I saw a photograph taken a century ago, a man in a suit lying awkwardly at the far side of the only unusual spot in a flat landscape where it's miles and miles from one tree or house to the next: a shallow small concavity, a sinkhole, perhaps twenty feet broad and not more than four feet deep at the center. The grand natural curiosity of that locale? The man is posing beside it, with more of the vacant expanse beyond him and in front of him than the rectangular photo could show, and so perhaps he has a greater sense of how truly odd and noteworthy the sinkhole is. He has brought his photographer all the way out from town to take the picture. It's his trophy. And it's something that would make the experienced traveler only laugh. It's not a something, but a kind of nothing. And yet once, at least, a man got down on his side, propped himself on his elbow, and held still for the camera, there…

I want to show you the fresh small tracks of the killdeer. On an afternoon of a breeze, after a black and green thunderstorm, when the torrents might have filled the ditch near our house and spilled into the yard so you couldn't tell anymore where the bank dropped off ten feet—on that kind of an afternoon, when the air seemed newly created and never yet used for anything, my mother might hand each of us a plastic bowl and say go across to the field and pick some dewberries and I'll make a cobbler for dinner. And don't track mud into the house when you come back! We crossed the ditch on the two-lane wooden bridge that was still there, then, before it was torn away and replaced with a wider, concrete one, with railings, and the name of some mayor.

I would need to forget that new bridge to get back to what I'm trying to see, and I'd need to remember that after big rains it was wonderful to lie belly-down on the wooden bridge, hang your head over the edge and watch the drowning murky flood go dizzying by. I'd have to forget that many years later I learned that the deep ditch around Mycenae was called Chaos.

On the other side of the ditch we entered the empty field by slipping through the rusty slack barbed-wire fence, and always cast a glance over at the ten or twelve good big trees in the next field beyond the berry field, a kind of grove, so strange in the wide emptiness. It was a mysterious place that we sometimes visited. Such a stadium of shade, so unnatural, seemed to have an elusive meaning. I wish I could show you the etched tracks of the killdeer, a bird that runs along the ground. Going to and from the grove, too, we'd find them beside the shallow slicks of rain on the flat bare sun-bleached earth, in the wide spaces between clumps of wiregrass and yaupon bushes. And in the berry field, around the mounds of tangled stickerbushes where the dewberries grew wild, heavy and freshened by rain. We rarely came close to a killdeer, but sometimes one would cry off taking flight ahead of us as we tramped.

To us those tracks were a hushing, stopping proof of wildlife as much as the sight of a lion would have been, and the sharp-scented air made us alert for every such trace as we picked berries and got tiny blood scratches on our wrists and hands. It was possible to spot a hornytoad, too, or some kind of small snake, *stay out of its way.* The breeze would fail after a while, and as soon as the air was still and warm again the bugs would return up into it. We could pick quarts of berries in a short time and they cooked down so much we needed to get a lot, and then we'd run back and deliver them, and wait for dinner and dessert.

I'd like to have stayed behind, though, just once, till the others were through the fence, back over the bridge, and gone, and then to have lain down beside the small rain slick with my white plastic bowl of black berries, next to the killdeer's pronged footprints, and told my photographer to open the shutter on me there.

My Dream of Bill

About two weeks after Bill died, while I was sleeping I saw that I was at dinner in a restaurant with others. Bill too was at the table. He was dead; but alive again except that his eyes remained squinted closed, and he looked bad. He talked animatedly, with anger and happiness, the others seemed amused, not a person remarked on his coming back. He was dead, though, and his body showed signs of decay. His face was leathery. It was a horror, but no one seemed to think his being there was horrible. I couldn't understand this.

He came again the following night—again we were eating at the restaurant. But Bill showed further damage, his skin yellow and stained and his hair reddish and long and dirty, and him talking even more animatedly, dominating the conversation (as he didn't do when alive), and the others again only amused, no one horrified, inexplicably, but me. Maybe they don't see that he is dead? But I know.

In the second restaurant scene something happened, I've forgotten what it could have been, and Bill, with hair now long and reddish, and his face a kind of dried-up leathery red, his eyes squinted entirely shut, began to talk faster and faster, with incredible energy (about what, I didn't remember even the morning after the dream) and then, in the sudden, instantaneous manner of dreaming, we were elsewhere, and Bill turned into other things. Persons, I guess. It wasn't Bill at all. Was it a spirit of which he was

63

an inextinguishable part—and of which others were parts, of which everything is a part? Is everything?

This spirit into which he changed was transformed through a hundred shapes in as many seconds. It was a power beyond Bill's. (But I couldn't recall, the next morning, whether they were forms of animals or persons or things or beings never seen.) We were outside now, on a high pleasant grassy place, with prospects and vistas. When the changes stopped, a kind of tall youthful harlequin was standing where Bill had been—gaily dressed and gay; laughing.

The harlequin, holding his audience, bent down to pick up from the perfect grass a tiny sequin of a jewel. Perhaps I had been the first to see it glittering in the grass and I had asked him what it was. He comes near me, and bends and picks it up. I didn't touch it because it was so bright, blue-white, that I can't look straight at it, it will hurt my eyes. The harlequin picked it up between thumb and forefinger, and, smiling, tossed it in the air with a snap of his wrist, upward. It rises, it soars on a long curve up into the sky, growing larger and even brighter and it becomes the sun.

The harlequin says something like, "That's what Bill came from."

And since I first wrote down my memory of that dream, about two weeks after Bill died, it has come back to me in many waking moments, and each time I have thought that I need to write it down not only for myself, in the airless chambers of my journals where only I speak and where I alone listen. Because I'd like to know: Has anyone else seen that harlequin? Would you write to me if you have?

No Matter What
Has Happened This May

 I love the little row of life along the low rusted
gardenwire fence that divides my small city backyard from my neighbor's. The wild unruly rose, I hacked like a
weed last spring; then it shot quick running lengths of vine in
every direction and shuddered into a thickness of blown blossoms
—the kind you can't cut and take in because they fall apart—so I
think I should cut it back as if to kill it again. The violets, just
beautiful weeds. Then there are yellow-green horseradish leaves,
they rose as fast as dandelions in today's rain and sun; and the
oregano and mint are coming back, too, you can't discourage
them. Last year's dry raspberry canes are leaning, caught in the
soft thorns of the new, at the corner. And beyond them, the mostly
gone magnolia in the widow's yard, behind ours, the white petals
on the ground in a circle like a crocheted bedspread thrown down
around the black trunk.

I went out to see what the end of the day was like, away from
everything, for a minute, and it was drizzling slowly. I touched
the ground, just to feel it wet against my palm; and the side of the
house, too. It was quiet, and I saw two robins bringing weeds and
twigs to a nesting place in the new leaves at the stumpy top of a
trimmed buckeye limb. How little they need—weeds and some
time—to build with.

In a month I may find a new one not yet fully fledged, lost
from the nest, and put it on the highest limb I can reach, but not
high enough to escape harm's way, I imagine, when the harm is a

shock within it, a giving up already; and it will be dead before morning. That's happened before. But these robins were just building, and one came with a full beak and paused a moment on a lower branch and cocked its head and looked upward and shifted as if it were a muscled cat, of all things, about to leap, and then it did leap and disappeared into the clump of leaves, and shook them, as the single drops of rain were gently shaking them one by one, here and there.

I was getting wet but I felt held outside because I could hear, from inside the house, a woman and a child—my wife and my daughter—laughing in the bathtub together, their laughter not meant for me but brought out to me like a gift by the damp still air so I could see that like the rain and the robins and the row of weeds they too were working and building. I'm not going to mention, now, any harm or hurt they have suffered; no winter nor summer government; no green troops nor trimmed limbs of trees; no small figures beaten or fallen. I wiped the dirt off my palms and I picked up again the glass of wine I had carried out with me. I rejoiced. There was no way not to, wet with the sound of that laughter and whispering in the last light of a day we had lived.

All-Out Effort

 I have cleaned off the old radio and put new bat-
teries in it. I have brought up the old boots from
the basement and cleaned and polished them. I have brought the
old rocker down from the attic and repaired the arm that was broken. I have washed and ironed the old khaki pants and the old soft
green shirt that were hanging at the back of the closet for so long.

Out the kitchen door, on the back landing, three floors above
the trash cans filled with this week's garbage, I've put the rocker,
I've set the radio down beside it and turned it on softly to the right
music, I've put on the pants and shirt and boots, I have sat down
in the neighborhood afternoon in the quiet time just before the
working day is going to end.

To prepare myself, I brought back to mind the unseeable
green of a meadow where we stood at night one time, where we
could see the reassuring lights and sounds of a crowded lit room,
and no one could see us: that moment, and others like it.

I've brought back to my mind the words I said to you, and
I've spoken them again, wearing these same clothes that I wore
then. Many times I have had lots of ideas and I started off with
many thoughts, but none of them was able to reach a resting
place, or find what I was after. Even though I chose a summer
day for this, or it chose me, I know enough to know this green
shirt may not be warm enough, because there are frozen fields
and cold streets to cross, just as many of them as of those furnace

nights buzzing outside with cicadas and tree frogs, sirens and shouts and engines.

But I'm wading and flying, now, I'm off, I'm headed into a place of ago, the radio's getting fainter, a little wind of time is starting to whip my pants legs and sleeves and make my eyes smart. Let the tears come! This rocker is gathering some speed. I'm going back, I'm going to rescue all of it!

About the Author

Poet, prose writer, translator, and critic, Reginald Gibbons has published several books of poems, most recently *Maybe It Was So* (University of Chicago, 1991). He has received fellowships from the Guggenheim Foundation and the National Endowment for the Arts. Gibbons currently lives in Evanston, Illinois, where he teaches at Northwestern University and serves as editor of *TriQuarterly* magazine.

Design by Ken Sánchez. Text set in Bembo by Thomas and Kennedy Typographers, Seattle, Washington. Printed on acid-free paper and Smyth sewn by Malloy Lithographing, Inc., Ann Arbor, Michigan.